D0099025

International Praise for *Love*

"It's slim, but it seems like it couldn't be any other way. . . . The effect caused by *Love*, the intellectual and emotional journey its readers go through, leaves them panting, their hearts beating hard."

—Gili Izikovich, *Haaretz*

"[*Love*] is written with stunning talent."

—Dan Miron, *Haaretz*

"I was astounded by its rhythm. . . . I felt I could hear the book's music or tone even in my sleep."

—Dror Mishani, author of the Avraham Avraham series, winner of the 2014 Bernstein Prize

"By using a hard-boiled language, corporeal, brutal, on the one hand, and soft and refined and almost unbearably intimate on the other, Eitan blurs the distinction between sex done under circumstances of love, romance, consent, and that done in a barter—of money, authority, ownership. When the two languages meet, stunningly beautiful moments are created. . . . *Love* is an anti-story about the impossibility to tell one story solely. Presenting a variety of narrative possibilities, Eitan subverts . . . the ambiguity of memory and the tyranny of the one story."

—Elad Bar-Noy, *Yediot Aharonot*

"[This] short and powerful novel by Maayan Eitan is winning quite a lot of attention recently. . . . Its unique literary qualities, its stylistic perfection, its unheard-of originality, should win [her] this kind of attention. *Love* is a once-in-a-lifetime novel, filled with urgency and mind troubling."

—Ruby Namdar, author of *The Ruined House*, winner of the 2013 Sapir Prize

"This is a small masterpiece. . . . Eitan presents a convincing world using seemingly realistic tools and allows the horror to attack it from the inside, achieving a nightmarish-surreal effect. She deceives, on purpose. The deception acts like some kind of vengeance, in language and in the story and especially in the readers, who are also partners to what cannot be written about but only around. The voyeuristic readers. Beautifully written, like a tax report. Like a knife."

—Ilana Bernstein, author of *Tomorrow We Will Go to the Amusement Park*, winner of the 2019 Sapir Prize

Love

Love

Maayan Eitan

PENGUIN PRESS   NEW YORK   2022

PENGUIN PRESS
An imprint of Penguin Random House LLC
penguinrandomhouse.com

Originally published in Hebrew as אהבה (*Ahavah*) by
Resling Books, Tel-Aviv.

LIBRARY OF CONGRESS CATALOGING-IN-PUBLICATION DATA

Names: Eitan, Maayan, 1986– author, translator.
Title: Love / Maayan Eitan.
Other titles: Ahavah. English
Description: New York: Penguin Press, 2022. |
    "Originally published in Hebrew by Resling Publishing"
Identifiers: LCCN 2021013462 (print) |
    LCCN 2021013463 (ebook) |
ISBN 9780593299692 (hardcover) |
    ISBN 9780593299708 (ebook)
Classification: LCC PJ5055.2.I855 A7513 2020 (print) |
    LCC PJ5055.2.I855 (ebook) | DDC 892.4—dc23
LC record available at https://lccn.loc.gov/2021013462
LC ebook record available at https://lccn.loc.gov/2021013463

Printed in the United States of America
1st Printing

Designed by Alexis Farabaugh

33614082806075

To Naama Tsal,

who was my beloved editor

And I finally decided that God formed a vile creature when He made woman, and I wondered how such a worthy artisan could have deigned to make such an abominable work which, from what they say, is the vessel as well as the refuge and abode of every evil and vice.

Christine de Pizan,
The Book of the City of Ladies

I:

Words Are Whores

You didn't
have any friends

You had a terrific laugh. You had long legs, big
tits, a flat belly. No, you were fat. You came
from ruined homes, well-off families, your parents were madly in love with each other. Your
father was an accountant, a kibbutz member,
homeless, a linguistics professor at a university. He loved you like his youngest daughter.
You were an only child. You were born to a
large family, after years of treatments, you
were adopted. Immigrated from Ethiopia. You
were good at math, you majored in accounting.
Hebrew literature. Kinesiology. You wanted to
work with children, become a lawyer, your

mother was a drug addict (sobered up without help), your uncle was a doctor. No, he was in jail, for attempted murder. You were blond, in summer the ends of your hair were bleached white. No; your hair was as black as a raven, and curly. You were born in Saint Petersburg. No no: your parents came from America, you were born in the suburbs, you replied to them in Hebrew when they talked to you in a jumble of foreign languages. You spoke Russian until you were seven then you forgot it, the snow too. You knew no other language but Hebrew. You refused to answer your grandparents when they spoke Amharic to you. You pretended not to understand them. Your father, the accountant, raped you in his office. Your grandmother kept the key from the '48 war. You were the good granddaughter, the prettiest girl in school, you had eyes that turned violet when you were angry, that you made sure to close on your first kiss. You had sex. You never came. No! You came every single time. You hated swallowing but did it anyway. You liked it so much you stopped in the middle to run to the bathroom and stick your fingers down your throat just so you could taste him again. You spat. Two months later you jumped off a high-rise. You were admitted to a psychiatric hospital. You arrived at the ER with low electrolytes and acute liver failure, but they pulled you back right from the edge. Lucky you. You spent a week in the ICU, then returned. Now you had money. You bought nice clothes. Toys for your nephews and nieces. Sponges so you could work through the month, without stopping. When you ran into each other in the car—someone getting in, someone out—you didn't smile. You laughed. Your laughter was so loud that your neighbors got sick of it. You pretended to moan while you wept miserably. You wept miserably. When you returned home and removed the makeup from your face it blended with tears of happiness. When you went out with your childhood friends you ordered cheap drinks, then more expensive ones. You didn't have any friends. You had a boyfriend who was a computer programmer and you worked only when he was on reserve service, or abroad for work, and you talked of getting pregnant but you were on the pill and didn't tell him. You liked women. You liked men. A lot. You didn't like anybody. You were pretty, you had normal skin, freckles, chapped lips, and you clipped your nails until your fingers bled because you were afraid that you might hurt someone. You didn't want to hurt anybody. You wanted to kill them all, you wanted to shout, one time you screamed. But it was a mistake and you did not repeat it. You kept your mouth shut. You had sex in public restrooms, dance clubs, on the steps of the lifeguard tower on the beach, in a luxury hotel, in your own bed. You got in the car that waited for you in the evenings with the same ease that you got out of it in the morning. What did you have to lose? You didn't have anything.

I said a blonde!

In the entrance to the first room stood a heavy, short man with a towel wrapped around his body and said, I don't believe it, I asked for a blonde. I tossed my hair (dark) while he pressed his fat fingers to his telephone screen. I tried to keep an impartial expression. Who knows, we might have to meet again. In the meantime he said, I told him a blonde! and turned away from me. (Mary had a little lamb, I hummed, little lamb, little lamb.) I smiled respectfully, turned around, and got out of there. Sergei, in the car, looked at me. If he wanted to ask something he did not ask. I sipped from

the plastic bottle I filled with arak before I
went out, wiped my lips with the back of my
hand and laughed, Assaf told him he's getting
a blonde. Sergei giggled and reached for my
bottle. The street was dark, and we waited. I
stroked the book that I put in my bag and did
not pull it out, because there are times in life
when you have to escape happiness. I checked
my email on my phone, sent another apology
to a friend who said she had something impor-
tant to tell me. Sergei's music, K-pop, roared in
my ears. His wife (he told her he's started to
guard a construction site at nights, or a park-
ing lot, a profitable job, and did not look at
her) surely pushes away the two children who
snuck into their queen-size bed, they got them
their own beds in the spare room, they should
learn to sleep by themselves already, and still
the kids insist on joining them in their bedroom. But Sergei's with me now, and we still
have long hours before morning. Sometimes
later than morning. If I'm getting two hundred

an hour, I thought, and half of it goes to Assaf via Sergei, how much does Sergei make? He left the radio and looked at me. He didn't seem discontented. I looked ahead, beyond the car glass, through the hedges to the villas, maybe I could see something. Someone, I imagined, stands in a darkened room and stares at me. I straightened my back. I reapplied the lipstick that was smeared by the alcohol. I tried to imagine how I would look if I were blond. While we waited for a new address from Assaf Sergei asked how long have I been doing this, and told me again about his wife and two kids, a boy and a baby girl, and he told her it was an excellent job, time passes, and she looked at him. The car was hot and I said, You don't mind if I take off my nylons, do you? Be my guest, he answered, and looked at his telephone screen while I twisted in the passenger seat and took off my stockings, fourteen ninety-nine on sale in the store, last chance, no returns and no refunds, but I never pay for these things anyway. Lib-by Lib-by, Assaf sang in my ears when I called to check if there were girls needed and told him my name. And she is mi-mine, Lib-by, Li-li-lib-by. Do you have kids, I asked in a voice that sounded pretentious to me too. Too high. What, only parents know this song, it seemed to me that I could detect caution in his voice, anger maybe. No, of course not, I answered. I don't know why, but I wanted him to like me. So what do you say, do you need a new girl or not?

Assaf

Assaf didn't ask to meet me. Already that same night I met Sergei, then Dima, Yehuda, another driver whose name I'd forgotten, Yair, maybe? Three, or five, or seven others with whom I slept every night, sometimes twice, sometimes night after night, it depends on who's working, or if they asked for me, but I didn't meet Assaf, and he didn't ask to meet me. I felt sorry. I wanted him to look at me.

You're not pretty

Libby is not a good name, said Karin when I introduced myself to her. No one will want you. She was even skinnier than me and wore platform high heels and spoke quickly and when I looked at her I saw a spark of true madness in her eyes, unlike me, unlike who I imagined I was. She looked at me from the front seat. I knew exactly what she was thinking. You're cute, but let me come up with a different name for you. (You're not pretty, I thought while she scrutinized me, and also, what are you doing here?) She stared at me for a short moment. Bar, she decided. Get me

Assaf on the phone, she ordered Sergei, we should tell him, with a name like Libby no one will want her. Sergei groaned. He had two kids at home and a wife to feed and he didn't have the energy, but he had plenty of time, so he put Assaf on the speakerphone and Assaf yelled at Karin and told her to shut up and sang, Her name is Libby, and she is mimine, Libby Libby Libby, Sergei joined him with a heavy accent, and that was it. I became Libby.

Men looked at me

They stared at me when I sat alone in the cafés, searched for my eyes when I walked past them in the street. They called me names: sweetheart, love. They kissed me with their eyes closed and stroked my face with their fingertips. I pushed my body against theirs, held their flesh, told them my secrets. They didn't want to hurt me. I am not strong. You never know how much I could suffer. I wore my ring on a thin chain around my neck. At first I felt its absent weight on my finger, then I forgot about it. I found other things to do: wandering the city cafés with nothing to do, I pulled books out of my bag but did not read them. Men looked at me. If there was need for it they'd asked for my number, or leave theirs, but I preferred joining them, in their rooms. They cooked black coffee on the stove while I threw up the contents of my stomach in their bathrooms; recited poetry to me; we smoked together. Then we had sex, their stubble scratching my inner thighs, the house cat jumping around us. Their semen never had any flavor. I bit them. They didn't bite back. I waited for them to fall asleep before I got out of there. I'm not pretty. Men looked at me. They talked to me, stopped me on the street, in bars, in cafés. We spoke. They went to the world's top universities, wrote books, poetry. They came in my mouth, my ass, on my breasts and belly. Their come was thick and sharp, dark almost. I slowly gathered my clothes even though their eyelids were heavy and they weren't looking at me. Then I got out of there. Men looked at me. They stared at me, bared their teeth when they smiled to me. They had money; the whiskey we drank was well-aged; they had heavy carpets, large TV screens, clothes made of expensive fabrics. I nodded when they spoke. Any other reaction would have been impolite of me. I bought new clothes every day; thin, black silk tops that felt strangely chilly when they slipped across my belly as I took them off. I pocketed a bottle of perfume; I liked its name. I fell asleep with their arms around my waist, but my sleep was erratic, brief, and eventually I slipped from under their bodies, put on my clothes again, and got out of there. I am not pretty. At first I forgot their names; then the sight of their homes, their bodies, the things they told me. Finally I decided to go to the hospital. The money I had in my wallet was exactly enough for the disposable razor and the taxi fare. I tore the plastic apart with my teeth in order to take the blade out of it. I am not pretty. I returned the next morning. Men looked at me, smiled to me when I passed them on the street, said that I was pretty when I asked them. I was running out of money. The eye shadows I bought were expensive, the dresses, the high heels with the black, thin ankle straps. In cafés I ordered cheap drinks, then progressively more expensive ones. I ate only rarely. When my money was almost completely gone I looked for a job, but the food joints and big-business owners refused to hire me. I'm not pretty. Men looked at me. I walked them home arm in arm, I rode in their cars with them. They had goose bumps when I touched them. I'm through, I thought, I'm really through now. They fell in love with me. When I snuck out of their bedrooms at dawn I looked in their wallets. Before I took the blade out of the razor I checked which bus lines stop by the hospital. My silk blouses stuck, wet, to my wrists, and were completely ruined. I returned three days later. Men looked at me.

They bought me presents, gave me money. I laughed loudly when they complimented me. I'm not pretty. They slept with me, pouted when I didn't come. I wore lace-top nylons. When I returned home I showered or did not shower. Men looked at me. They touched me, pulled up the hem of my dress on the steps of the lifeguard tower on the beach. Winter will soon be here. When they left I stuck out my finger and drew long, deep lines in the sand. Then I put it in my mouth and chewed the sand that got stuck to it. It had no flavor. But men looked at me. They dedicated poems to me, books, text messages, newspaper articles, conceptual artworks. I am not pretty, but my movements are quick and my mind is sharp. So I didn't throw away the razor and also bought an antiseptic cream this time. When I ran out of savings I went to the desert, knocked on my father's door and asked him if I could stay there. He gave me a bed in my childhood room. Men looked at me. They slipped their hands down my back when they welcomed me, pricked up their ears when I talked to them. How long could I stay there. At night I read cheap paperbacks, long novels, everything I could lay my hands on. When I fell asleep my sleep was erratic, brief. I dreamed that men were looking at me. They ripped the nylons off my thighs, moved my silk underwear to the side. I felt nothing but the slight wind. On the beach I searched for mother-of-pearl shells, and found none. Seahorses hovered in midair. I closed my eyes. The waves had a salty sound and the sand, once again, didn't have any flavor. Something came in, left, and left something. Men looked at me. They rented rooms by the hour for me in the suburbs, gave me money, asked me: What is this thing. I changed my telephone number. I bit the tips of my fingers till they bled, my lips. I tried to come; I stuck to the appropriate level of honesty;

occasionally I sighed. Then I got out of there. Men looked at me. They were worried about me, paid for the coffee I ordered, tried again and again to talk to me. I smiled. I am not pretty. I swapped the black silk tops for a high-waisted leather skirt and sharp-heeled boots, clothes that I had slipped into my bag when one of the salesgirls wasn't looking; at midnight I got into the stranger's car with a sure foot. In the morning I returned to the café, my eyes free of makeup, and men looked at me. I looked back. I went with them to the matinee. *The reconstructions have been made as authentically as possible! The films have been made as authentically as possible!* When they shivered I put my hand on their hearts. After the movie we drank hot chocolate. I laughed. They looked at me and I saw that there was true affection in their eyes, the corners of their mouths. Even though I'm not pretty. The short skirt lay in my bag. Thirty minutes before midnight we said goodbye. I kissed them on their cheeks, laughed again because their stubble tickled me. Then I got out of there. In the mall restroom I tore the plastic off the disposable razors and changed my clothes.

Women also looked at me

They stared at me when I put out my cigarette butt in the molded plastic cup that served as an ashtray in the smokers' corner, when I paced, back and forth, in the empty white hallway that connected the shared bedrooms. What else could I do? Once a week they summoned me to their therapy rooms and talked to me, crossed the shin of their right leg over the shin of their left leg and their left leg over the right leg and sent me omniscient looks, so that I would tell them something. I didn't tell them anything. I laughed loudly when they asked if I felt any pain, where did it feel painful. What else could I do? I could have kissed them with my eyes closed, let them stroke my face, press my body to theirs, hold on to their soft flesh and only then tell them my secrets. But I didn't confess to them, even though I wanted to, sometimes. Though it wasn't an irresistible urge. When I finally went out on the streets again I pretended not to see that men were looking at me. If there was any need I would have looked back, mumbled something, an offer maybe, a sophisticated pun, something to show them I get it. That I'm no different. But they no longer interested me. The coffee they cooked was sour and if I wanted to I could have written better poems than they did. I thought about Assaf, whom I've never met. What is he doing now? How much is he making? How would I feel if I slept with him? What flavor is his semen? He would bite back if I bit him, I knew, and wouldn't let me leave so quickly. Even though I wasn't his type. I was none of their types. Despite the flats I made sure to wear I stayed as tall as they were, and always too thin. (There's not a gram of fat on your body, someone said when I tried to climb on his cock. It was a birthday gift, but he did too much coke before and couldn't get hard at all. I snorted two of his lines, took the money, and got out of there.) What else could I do? I got back in Sergei's car. While we waited for Assaf to send new addresses I learned to like some of Sergei's songs, there was one with strong bass sounds that made me feel like dancing, but the Volvo was too stuffy and small, and I was hardly drunk enough. Arak prices went up and I switched to vodka instead and diluted it with water. Sergei drove with confidence. Sometimes, under a traffic light, my chin pointing forward, I could see that he was looking at me.

Money

I saw Sergei more than anyone else, and it wasn't hard to like him. The money we shared between us accrued in a messy pile in my writing desk drawer. For a moment I thought about the bank cashier's curious gaze, the one trapped in cheap blue eye shadow, and decided I couldn't deposit it with them. The prices of vodka also rose, and once every couple of nights I needed new nylons, and condoms, and there was a special place that had period sponges on sale, so I bought them there. But the books I continued to read in the dead hours of night were lifted from the thick shelves at the mall when they didn't look at me, and the clothes were even easier to pilfer. The eye shadow I stole was the expensive one. I swapped my high heels, the nice shoes with the black, thin ankle straps, for a pair of sneakers, and only wore them later. Women looked at me while I removed them from my feet in their offices, twisting myself like in Sergei's car seat, or like a call girl strip-teasing in front of who-ever told her to. Though I didn't get a chance to do that, or I did and forgot about it. So while I rocked my legs in front of women whose diplomas lay in their writing desk drawers (Do they also write? What do they write?), I thought that had I told them my secrets, this is what I would have said to them: that I enjoyed how the wind tossed my hair when Sergei sped up on the highway, that I felt neither hot in summer nor cold in winter, and that with each passing night I turned more and more beautiful, so beautiful it was impossible not to look at me.

Small breasts,
like seashells

I continued to meet Karin in the car, and she continued to call me Bar, and I thought about the ads showing pale models that were hung on the new high-rises in the areas to which we were sent, prostrate in lace bras and underwear or lying in a bathing suit on the beach, their breasts bursting out of their arms. I didn't have patience for the way the lace irritated my skin, and finally I gave up my bra altogether. I wore the same clothes every night: a short leather skirt, a black top, nylons, underwear, sneakers. A thin silver necklace to my neck, my ring. But Karin shined. Every time I saw her she had a different costume on: once she was a schoolgirl. Once a high-end prostitute. Once loose sweatpants and a tight T-shirt with a décolletage so large that it was possible to see how round, beautiful, soft her breasts were. Mine were small. This is what I told Assaf the first time I called him, on a bench in the middle of a noisy boulevard, shielding the phone with my one hand so that he could hear me better: do you need more girls? Yes, I'm experienced. Brown. Dark. Fair skin. This number of centimeters on this number of kilograms. I'll be there. I muted my phone and went to see an art show in one of the new galleries in the south of the city, took a shower in the locker room of a nearby pool, put makeup on my face and ten minutes before midnight waited for the driver—Sergei, Assaf told me that was his name—to pick me up from the bus stop. Young men looked at me. They were beautiful. I wasn't interested in them.

You had secrets that did not interest me then, and later I regretted not listening better. We met in Sergei's old car, or Dima's, or Yair's, or Yehuda's, offering each other cigarettes, or chewing gum, or chocolate, or we passed each other in the hallways of the apartments we were sent to. We exchanged half smiles. Once when someone led me to his room I saw a foreign girl with slanted eyes crouching (she wore no lace bra, she wore no bra at all) on her knees. When I entered she raised her head, stared at me, then brought it down again. She's not one of Assaf's, I thought, though who knows. Another time someone was already waiting for me in a by-the-hour room, and when I undressed she said, you have a beautiful body, and I said, thank you, and looked at her. In the car

Karin spoke quickly, quickly, quickly. I thought that there's no way she's not high, or manic. Maybe both of them. Sergei yelled at her to shut up, that he can't think like that, he can't listen to his music, he can't hear Assaf on the phone, can't enter the new address on his GPS, that he can't work like that. At the new address only I got out. When I got back in the car she was already gone, Assaf had enough of her tonight, Sergei reported, he drove her back home. We have another address, we're late, get going, he told me. I wanted to ask him whether he's not tired, working like that at night, I wanted to ask him whether he was making enough money, I wanted to ask him whether he thought about what we did while he waited in the car, or what does he think of us, but I rolled down the window instead, combed out my hair that had lengthened, and began swaying to the sounds of music.

Men looked at me. They examined the size of my breasts, the circumference of my thighs, the color of my nipples, my dimples, everything that could have aroused in them attraction or disgust, even though I quickly learned that as long as you tell them you're eighteen and are willing to do everything, they wouldn't care much. So I did everything they told me to do, things I knew Karin and the others were doing, things that the men I liked didn't dare do to me. But this was what I said and Assaf made sure to define the boundaries of the deal: yes, she's very experienced, I imagined him saying. Fair skin, dark hair, small breasts but gorgeous, I'm telling you, and does everything. Ev-ery-thing.

Everything

Massaging, for example, the balls of a heavy ultra-Orthodox man from Bnei Brak while a beautiful blonde (I forgot her name) sucked his dick. I remember what he looked like and how many children he said he had (Eight. Ten. No, thirteen), but her name escapes me. She stared at him while she brought her lips close to his penis (I was glad that I wasn't the one who had to do it, but later she left and we stayed in the room together and there were still fifteen minutes left before the phone rang and Dima, this time, told me to get out of there, get going, there's another address), and she smiled at me and I smiled at her and he was drunk, dead drunk, finished, and we couldn't stop giggling above him, above his heavy, naked, furry body, my hand still on his balls, she wiping her lips with the back of her own hand, and when he rolled on his side and started snoring we laughed so hard that I was afraid we'd wake him, and she put on her clothes and said, Bye, I have to leave now, and continued to laugh until her eyes filled with tears, they were pale, blue or green, I think, and the man, whose checks bounced more than once (Cash only, ordered Dima before I left the car) and had eight children in Bnei Brak and once (said Sergei when I told him about it a few nights later) Yehuda had to come up and show him the gun he carried so that he would pay him first thing, pay Yehuda, not us, I mean the girls, and while outside men rode in their cars, and the stock market crashed and then rose again, and Sergei's kid smiled a coy smile when he stood at the door to his parents' bedroom

at midnight, inside the room the beautiful
blonde (Maria? Vanessa? Natasha?) gave head
to the fat Orthodox man while I rubbed his
balls and we laughed our hearts out because
he drank so much and had no clue, he didn't
have a clue about what we were doing there,
and then she left, he wanted to stay alone with
me, and I didn't see her again. Ever.

Then we drove back to the city and I laughed
hard in my heart because Dima was sullen
and didn't want to talk and in any case these
are not things you're supposed to laugh about
in the first place, but I laughed anyway. And
the sun rose and there were no new addresses
so I laughed all the way back home and I
laughed when I said goodbye to Dima (Till
soon, Dima) and I laughed in the stairway
and when I put the key in the door lock and
when I took off my clothes and changed to a
large T-shirt and sweatpants (the leatherlike
skirt made me laugh, the nylons, the expensive black underwear thrown on the writing
desk, I laughed so hard), and I laughed in my
bed and when I tried to fall asleep I laughed

till I thought I would choke and die in my sleep, and the coroner would write under the relevant clause—cause of death: laughter, the deceased (a young woman in her late twenties, identifying marks: a tattoo or two, a childhood scar, a strange lip spasm) laughed until she was suffocated by her own laughter, and this thought only made me laugh harder and when I fell asleep I dreamed that I laughed so hard that the window glass shattered and plaster fell off the walls and the apartment collapsed into itself and the building fell down, burying the tenants who got up to work while I slept and laughed, and slept and slept and laughed, and Karin and the blonde and the one with the slanted eyes and the others joined me, why not, there's room, there's demand, and Sergei, and Dima, and three, or five, or seven every night, and Assaf joined us too while he counted the money, and he counted and he laughed, and counted and counted and laughed, and all the men laughed with him and we laughed, everywhere around the world we laughed, and if you joined us and laughed you'd be saved, and if you cried you died, I repeat: if you cried, you died.

Heroin. You want some?

Yes. I want some.

Every night I get in the car ten minutes before midnight and the driver, Sergei or Yehuda or Dima or Yair, starts the engine. It's early, usually we don't have to rush anywhere. We wait for an address. I ask him to stop by one of the stores to buy more arak, or gum, or razors. We argue about the music. I want something loud, they want something in Hebrew, we reach a compromise. Karin talks quickly as usual. Yael says something about her studies. How long have you done this for? And you? The car goes. Rain beats down. Someone goes in, someone gets out. There's an address. Assaf calls and says that another car is waiting for me. The driver looks familiar, but I don't feel like conversing this time. I do what I'm told to do. Riders on the storm, I hum.

Into this house we're born, into this world we're thrown. What else could I do? I needed time to pass somehow. I open the door and slam it behind me. Hey! says the driver. I turn to him and smile a sweet smile. I'm sorry. After an hour exactly I come back, careful when I get inside this time. We count the money. A lot. My wallet swelled up. The writing desk drawers burst from papers and money I had nothing to do with. I got in the car and I got out of it. I sucked men's dicks. I climbed on men's dicks. I bit their necks gently. I let them bite me. I moaned when they hit me. Back in the car I showed Sergei (or Yehuda, or Yair) the marks on my body. I got out of the car and I got into it. We drove. Sergei left after two weeks and returned after three. Someone new replaced Karin who suffered, or so I heard, a psychotic episode. I had chlamydia but I took care of it. The family doctor warned me with an embarrassed smile about unprotected sex, she said that a lot of young men don't take precautions today and that I should protect myself. I protected myself, I stayed away from young men. In the early hours of morning on the highway one of the new drivers turned on the stereo at a deafening volume. I opened the window and the ends of my long hair slapped my face in the wind hard. Your golden hair, I recited, your ashen hair. I didn't cut it this time. I got in the car. The car traveled. I got out of it.

Whore

We lied to our parents. We lied to the law. We lied in cheap restaurants, we lied in bars, we lied in factories for assembling aluminum tools, our hands moving skillfully on the assembly line. We lied to the university, we wrote them: I come from a poor background. My parents are state workers. Please give me a scholarship so that I can learn a profession. We lied to our best friends. We had best friends. We lied to them. We lied to our husbands. We didn't tell them where the money came from. No, we didn't tell them we had any money. We told them we don't have any. But the money piled up. Our makeup dresser drawers (we didn't have a writing desk; that was a lie. We didn't write) filled with new bills every night. We didn't tell our nieces and nephews where the toys we bought them came from (we lied in the toy factories, we lied when we said that there were toy factories, we lied when we wrote. We didn't write). We lied when we wrote letters to the income tax offices. To university administrators. We lied to our husbands. We didn't have husbands. We lied to them. We lied to our pimps. Our lies were wiped off our lips like the blue eye shadow on the china dolls' eyelids in the factory. Listen to me: I grew up in a train car. No, I'm not kidding, a train car. They had to get a crane to bring it to the wadi (in Hebrew: ravine, valley) and put it in the dried-up riverbed. The year was nineteen-eighty-eight. They pumped the water from a nearby well (Hebrew: thieves) and for electricity they used a generator. My father weeded the wild thorns. My mother gave birth and gave birth until she couldn't anymore, and at night we spread blankets on the floor and slept on them. Two adults and four babies. No, I'm lying again: two babies and four adults. Or half-half. Never mind; my mother milked the goats so she could give the milk to my father and us (a strong press on the goat's udder, the smell of sweat and sex and the dirt of the chickens that ran to and fro on the balcony. What balcony? I'm not lying, there was a balcony). We wandered around barefoot and naked. The train car took off every night. Who does the world belong to? Us. My father bought a herd of cattle. Four hundred of them! The first word I learned was *primipara* (the smell of sweat and sex and burned meat rose from their bodies, a bad smell against the green smell of the weeds in the wind). We marked them with a branding iron. I'm not lying! Our money ran out. My sisters and I stole bread slices from the dining room of the nearby kibbutz. We had lice, their movement was delightful when they shaved our long hair, that earlier shone in the sun, to the scalp. Let it be a lesson! In the train car they assembled a small kitchen. The farm was a haven. But don't trust them. The cows, we slaughtered. No: we sent them away, so others will slaughter them. We smiled. We learned how to sew, we danced. The curtains flew in the heat, the wind. We ran after each other in the yard, the mountains, in the dried-up riverbed (thieves, where is the water?). We had all that we could think of. Dolls that stared at us with their china eyes (we lied in court, in school, we lied to our husbands). Books to read (the first words I learned: *Shhhhh, don't worry, everything will be all right*). They protected us. The army came and protected us. We were respectful. Thank you, Father. Thank you, Mother. They loved us. Thank you, soldier. We grew up. Our feet turned a little inward. It'll pass before you're married, said the doctor they sent us to. Thank you, Doctor. Don't let the boys do that to you, said the kindergarten teacher (everywhere our feet stepped on we loved, everywhere they loved us. Who does the land belong to? Us), so you'll be able to get pregnant later. Thank you, kindergarten teacher. Do you want to work tomorrow? said Assaf. I got my period, I told him (did I lie? I didn't lie this time). There's a place that sells cheap sponges to the girls, the driver can take you, your choice though, he answered. I'm in, I answered.

One, two, three, four. Seven, eight. At the end
of each night I counted them because I did not
want to forget them. There was Karin who
spoke quickly and gave me chewing gum. The
Russian with the blond hair who told me I
have a beautiful body, and it was sweet of her,
and when the fat, hairy drunk to whose room
we were sent together fell asleep we dressed
quietly, giggling, and left, never even consider-
ing to look in his wallet to take more than we
deserved. This was what I deserved: to be
whipped on the buttocks, to be licked in my
pussy, to be suckled on my nipples (erect, erect),
to be told: Come for me. I came. I am not lying!
The fingers of a young, educated, and wealthy
man inside my body, while with the other hand
he pulls my hair and whispers in my ear: You

47

deserve it, don't you? I deserve it. I also counted
Yael, the Ethiopian, who had three classes to
finish before she could graduate. She majored
in Latin America and history. I wanted to remember her. She was so beautiful I couldn't
stop looking at her. When we said goodbye (she
went into the apartment hotel; I stayed with
Sergei, then another driver for an inter-city ride
to meet a businessman from Brazil, like they
promised in the ads, to seduce us, you must be
kidding me! There was no need to seduce us at
all). I thought about happiness, how there are
times in life when you can only escape it. Fuck
that, I told Sergei. Play something else on the
radio, give me more arak, you want a cigarette?
I knew that he wanted to ask me why I'm doing
it, but I didn't want to tell him. Why am I doing
it? Because I feel like it.

Why did I do it

The truth was I became addicted to the smell of mold in the showers of narrow hotel rooms, to the hardly cleaned towels, to the cheap perfume Karin used, to Maria's sweet face, or Yael, or Natasha, to the curious look in the eyes of lawyers, doctors, high school janitors, bike-rental-store owners when they saw me. As if they expected someone different. Prettier? No no, different. And still they agreed to have sex with me, to insert their fingers in my genitals, to look at themselves in the mirror while they fucked me, to come in my mouth, my vagina, on my face, my ass and breasts. The smell of come stuck to me. It wasn't completely foreign. I looked at the night sky as it was seen through the window, I looked at the sight of bodies in the mirror, and I did all they told me to do, then more than that.

What is your name

Every night someone gets in the car and someone gets out of it. Gum exchanges hands. Bills
in the glove compartment, the smell of cheap
shampoo in the hair (Did you have time to
shower? How did you have time to shower?),
sand stuck to the shoe heels, the spark of as-
phalt after rainfall. Someone gets in the car,
then someone else gets out of it. What is your
name? And yours? Pretty name. Music in a foreign language, Sergei enters another address
into the GPS. Someone gets out, someone gets
in. What is your name? Pretty name. Is it your
real name? No. Yours? No. Want some gum?
Thank you. Want a cigarette? How old are you?

And you? Someone gets in. Arak? Vodka? A cigarette? Where are we going? What time is it now? Yes, I had time. How long have you done this? A year, and you? Someone gets in the car, someone gets out of it. Five months. How old are you? Eighteen. You? Eighteen. Is that your real name? No. And yours? Someone gets in, someone out. Can I have some gum? Do you want a cigarette? The car goes. How long have you done this? Don't know. And you? A month. What is your name? Libby. And yours? Margarita. Someone get in, I get out.

You again?

Me.

Blond, I said!

I'm not blond.

You're okay? Are you any good at it?

I'm good at it.

In the morning's pale light (I imagine) someone stands and looks at a young woman sleeping, her messy hair covering her face. He puts
on his clothes, kisses her on her cheek and
says: Bye, sweetheart. I myself didn't have any
time for stuff like that. I returned the knife (I
imagined) to its place in the kitchen drawer (I
was sent to a residential apartment; I did not
wash the blood off of it) and looked back at
myself in the mirror, naked, hair unkempt,
and not very pretty. The man lay with his face
to the ceiling and if he was able to open his
eyes he'd probably notice three deep stabs, one
between the ribs, another one in the heart (am
I imagining?), the third reaching the center of
his right lung. I found two hundred dollars on

the kitchen table, put on my clothes, and got out of there. I didn't have anything else I could do, but do it a second time. This, in any event, was what I told them.

Why did I do it

—Because he deserved it.

—Because I was bored.

—Because it was a revenge.

—Revenge on someone I loved.

—I didn't love anybody.

—He was fat. I didn't like it.

—The knife stared at me from the utensil drawer. The utensil drawer was closed. It stared at me. It's only hard to kill someone the first time, then you get used to it. I read about it in a book, or saw in a movie, but I believed it.

—The blade first pierces the layers of skin, then the veins, the tendons, the flesh, everything falls apart to my touch, with my movement. It's addictive, I swear. I read it in a book, or I saw it in a movie, and believed it.

—My knife, I returned it to the utensil drawer with my fingerprints. They'll find me. They'll ask:

—Why did you do it? and I'll say:

—The truth was that I liked it (or I wrote that I liked it, or I wrote).

Fifteen minutes before I have to get back in the car the driver calls me. Libby, he says, fifteen minutes. Okay, I say and hang up. There's a smell of something burnt in the air, and I don't think about anything specifically, because why think when you're being fucked. Fuck this, I say to myself, fuck everything, and take out a small bag with heroin. When he finishes I go to the bathroom and wipe myself. Then I get back in the room; five minutes later I'm outside, dizzy. There's a big bloodstain on my shirt, is it blood? I think. No, I don't think anything. I need a new shirt, I tell the driver. Shit, I can see him staring at me. What happened to you? I don't know, I say, drive me home please. The sun rises when I climb to the last floor and sit on my building roof's ledge. Am I still bleeding? I don't know, what am I thinking about? I think about birds, I think about ghosts, I think about the smell of poppy seed cakes that just came out of the oven and I make sure there are at least seven floors below me before I jump. On the sidewalk I brush off the gravel and some glass shards that stuck to my knees and get up. Is everything okay? asks a passerby. Everything's fine, I answer.

II:

Love

I called you

I called you love and I called you baby and I
called you puppy and I called you master and
I called you daddy. I called you home and I
called you to my bed and I called you when
I showered and I called you in my sleep and
I called you and asked whether you liked my
body and if my breasts please you and is my
nose straight enough. I stroked you with the
tips of my fingers. I stroked your dick with the
tips of my fingers. I tickled you. I called you
love and I called you sweetheart and I cooked
pasta for you and cleaned my apartment spe-

cial before you came and I rolled restlessly from side to side in my sleep until you woke up and hugged me. I moved in with you. I called you love and my sweetheart and I did all I could so you'd know nothing and sometimes I lied to you. I asked you whether my breasts really did please you. I called you sweetheart. They're killing me, I mumbled in my sleep, and I knew you heard me. I called you love. I baked cakes for you and cooked you pasta. I didn't tell you what I did when I stayed out all night. You did not ask me. Summer passed. I called you love, love, and when you didn't answer I called you daddy and I called you master. I shaved myself. I promised I liked it. I lied to you. I promised I liked it and asked you to come on my face and begged you to fuck me. I called you daddy and I called you master. I made efforts for you to not leave me. Daddy, I never knew you were, this much. I went through your box of letters. I discovered, one by one, your secrets. I promised you I'll remember everything that you've forgotten. Only those who remember live eternally, so I never died. But I forgot that I lied. I forgot you were lying to me.

Why did you stop
doing it?

The truth was I got tired. No, the truth was
that my body itched all the time, and I had
urinary tract infections and I felt I've had
enough in general, so I stopped answering Assaf's calls, and then I changed my telephone
number again and enrolled in school because
I needed to find something else to do, and on
the lawn I met somebody. I told him. No, I
didn't tell him. But he called me a whore anyway. When he fucked me. Or maybe he didn't
say that, and I only imagined. I was good at it.
At what? Imagining. I thought about a lot of
other things, like the life I wanted to have

then. In that life I felt very contented. I had a husband who worked for the government and a moment before thirty I got pregnant, because there are times in life when you have to hold on to happiness by its two horns and ride it. Sometimes, when we slept together, always very gently, I remembered. So I told him, I was very honest, I'm remembering now, and he hugged me. It was particularly sweet, because in the end torments must warrant themselves too, and love has to cure you. So I was cured. No, I pretended to be. I found new things to do, and forgot that I once used to do other things but when Assaf's number appeared on my screen I remembered there was another small thing that I wanted to ask Yael, or Yarden, or Karin, and to overcome the urge to reply I found more and more things to do, and started working in an office where they did not look at me often and I could pretend I was one of them. During breaks, sometimes, I took out a small knife and cut my inner thigh in the restroom. It was also boring, but I got over it. I went to bed not too late. My husband was promoted and the child grew, what child? The one that I had with him. Because something had to be done. Or this was how I imagined it. Because the truth was that when I finally answered his call Assaf said that you should never stop playing a winning card and mine is a joker, so I did not stop doing it.

How long did you do it

Three or four months, and not continuously,
it's difficult to remember things like that. Two
months (not continuously) when I was a child,
I mean, sixteen. This is how he remembered
it: he told the girl to undress and sat on the
bed and jerked off in front of her. The girl was
six. I mean sixteen. Twenty-six. I mean, she
wasn't a girl anymore. He spat on her. This is
how I remembered it: he told her to lie down
on the bed and stood over her. His eyes stared
into her eyes. She turned her head, then looked
back again. Spit trickled down from his lips to
her face. Her eyes. It didn't have any sound,

how can spit have a sound? This spit had it. A liquidy sound, and a very white one. She felt pressure in her bladder, but didn't say anything. What happened? He kissed her goodbye and closed the apartment door behind her. It was a by-the-hour room. No, it was an apartment. She leaned on the door and closed her eyes. When she opened them again at least ten years were gone and her long hair no longer passed her earlobes. With trembling fingers she knocked on the door. He welcomed her inside.

Love

The man who opened the door was older than me, but not by much. Maybe ten years. He only knew what I had told him: I'm not pretty. My nose is broken in two places (a childhood accident, and once someone hit me) and my pelvis is slightly tilted. In the foyer there was a small light, and it wasn't the first time we'd met. No, of course it was the first time we met, there were no other times, how could there be. In order to meet we needed nothing but our two bodies, and it was too easy and not very interesting. No, it fascinated me. In all honesty I don't remember. But I remember I loved him. How do you remember love? Just like that. The next time we didn't even need our bodies, we met because of the story, the words opened their mouths one after the other. But had we been smarter we would've known that you should also say the things one says on such occasions: I love you. And I love you. No, of course we said that. What we knew but decided to never tell each other were other things entirely, such as this is life, this is the world, we can't do anything we want to. I mean the things in the books we read. No, who am I kidding, we could have. We did them. But finally, when the morning light started showing, he still closed the door behind me. What could we do, we couldn't do anything. So how long did you do it? Every night.

What we did

We sucked men's dicks. We climbed on men's dicks. We bit their necks gently, or with force, depending on what they asked us to do. We let them bite our necks, nipples, hit us. We moaned, of course, when they hit us. Back in the car we showed Sergei, or Yair, or Yehuda the marks on our bodies. Sergei wasn't excited. We were, all of us, that is, who could have told if we weren't. Karin returned. One night when there were no new addresses Sergei went outside for a smoke, and we stayed alone in the car. She looked straight ahead. I looked at her. We were silent, what was there to say anyway?

There was nothing. Actually, we might have spoken. She might have told me to run away from there. Yes, she told me, run as long as you can now! It seems like I should have listened to her, but I stayed inside, this was what I imagined Assaf wanted me to do. Perhaps I didn't imagine. Perhaps, in the end, I met him. I think I fell in love with him, I think, in the end, that I fell in love with him. Or perhaps it was someone else. Who opened the door for me and wrapped his arms around me and pressed me to his chest. Who waited for me on a bench next to my building when I was delayed and asked, is everything all right? Everything's fine. Do you remember that I told you what we did? I lied. I made it all up for you. So that you love me.

In conclusion:

The police investigation revealed nothing, as did the private investigation led by Assaf, who then told me to leave, they didn't need me anymore. I laughed. I asked for one more night, the last one, and he gave it to me. I did not shine. The flesh was, as always, just flesh, one which you may and you may not touch. I touched it. It didn't bother me. How do you remember? Without much effort, or thought, when you tell someone something that could have happened in books, perhaps in a dream, in a fantasy, inside my head only. Listen to me: I once loved a man who wanted to kill me. In the end he found me blue and breathless and, laugh as much as you like, saved me. What happened in between? I don't remember. In any event when I regained my consciousness I left him. What could I do? I'd had enough then. How do you remember love? What a joke. You forget it.

Occasionally I remembered how one time after the other you promised me that you'll never touch another. I found out that, of course, you were lying. I thought about the things that we did to each other, and the things I imagined you'll go on doing to me. I whispered them in other men's ears. A lie. But there were always others, because the flesh may and may not be touched. I kept a knife in my bag. There were men who liked it, that I took it out and cut myself, naked and not very pretty, in front of them. Blood trickled down quietly. Between my thighs. Someone whips me with his belt, someone else holds me firmly, pressing my body to his. Together. How much can I suffer? I didn't mind it. Where were you? Home. In the early hours of morning I climbed up the stairs to the apartment we shared together. The building stood firm, and you, I knew, were sleeping. How can you sleep at night? You wanted me to have kids with you. We wanted to bring them together. That was the whole story: you and I against the whole world, each one and what they know about it. Or what they're good at. On weekends I went out dancing. I didn't ask you if you wanted to join me. You were angry. Men let me in their nightclubs. They looked at me dancing. I was interchangeably cold and bored and sometimes I burst out crying. No, I never cried, because there was no sadness in the world, only joy. That flooded me. What? I feel nothing, nothing, I feel nothing. When we slept together I imagined it was like soft cotton balls, no, like a couple of kittens, baby skin touch, like a slight wind blowing. I screamed. Everything made me noxious. And the touch of your hands most of all. No, I desired it. I couldn't sleep, how do they sleep? I wanted a different life. In that life I had someone who cared for me. Who waited awake at home while I worked out late, who happily ate the food I made him. It had the taste of home. As if we have a home, as if we lived in it, together. As if we'll never forget what we promised. You withdrew. I always never cried. But it was a life that suited me: yes, I could have lived it.

All that time you insisted you loved me, and never asked whether I loved you too. You got used to me, to how I looked in the morning, with messy hair and not very pretty, in your bed. Occasionally I told you I loved you too. Did I lie? I didn't lie then. I had more money than I could imagine and I had no real reason to go back to work, but I told you I got a new job, in a gallery this time. I described to you in detail how I do nothing for hours, sometimes speaking to the few visitors, sometimes selling them catalogs. The artworks were expensive. Large bronze sculptures that the wealthy kept in closed rooms, whose temperatures were kept meticulously. Without the sun's direct touch. As if they could save something. I should have gotten pregnant when it was still possible, I thought. I didn't tell you anything, because it was too late already. We ate in silence. You almost never looked at me. I wanted to scream. I sat with my back straight, quiet, very careful, sometimes frightened. What did I do? What did you know then? Once every few weeks I climbed up the stairs to the roof and passed one foot after the other off the edge. I didn't plan to jump, but I hoped you'd come out of the apartment and save me. I never told you how much I was afraid to die. I told you I was afraid of nothing.

In the end someone else came out of his room and stroked my hair and held me in his arms and pressed me to his chest and asked, is everything all right? Everything's fine, I told him. The night's quiet. Do you remember I told you what we did? I invented nothing and I never loved you at all because you forget love, I forgot it like others forget the milk out of the fridge or their keys inside the car, a lonely sock in the washing machine, the telephone number of the last guy who said he had fun with me, and I nodded seriously (another kind of behavior would have been considered disrespectful) while I banged my head hard against the wall, no, I threw my whole body against it, and the wall turned to me and said: What are you doing now? What exactly do you think that you're doing now? And I answered, I'm forgetting, don't interrupt me, and someone's voice was heard saying, I would have never broken up with someone who gives head like this, so I knew I gave him head but I didn't know when or where or whether he paid me (any other behavior would have been disrespectful) and I replied, Everything can be replaced, and me more than all.

In conclusion:

The police investigation resulted in nothing, because there was no one to start it. What happened? I once killed a man who loved me. Or the opposite. I was killed by a man I loved. I stole the gun from my father. He carried it for security reasons. But I never felt secure, so I shot him. Who? First of all, my father. Then my best friend. Then the man I loved, but the bullet missed the three targets, and I wasn't able to kill any of them, though I wanted to. What? To feel loved so much, and safe, and that I can't be replaced even though it's clear that I can be. This is how I imagine I'll show

up again at your door: instead of two suit-
cases I'll have a backpack this time. In the
backpack there would be a book, in the book
it would say, we are free women, said Anna to
Molly. Perhaps Molly to Anna. I decided to
become a free woman too, I had too much
money and I got sick of returning to your bed
every night, so free from the chains of this
world I called Assaf again and told him, Hey,
Assaf, it's Libby. Assaf replied in short, con-
cise sentences. He told me to dress nicely, and
that tonight he will pick me.

You got a fast car,
I want a ticket

Assaf waited in a white Honda. Not particularly new. What's up with Karin? I wanted to ask. I didn't ask it. Instead I tried to examine him. It was dark. But what's it about me? I wanted to ask again. I didn't ask it. The car slid through the night. Where are we going? When will we get there? Earlier on the telephone Assaf told me to bring my money. All of your money, he emphasized, bring it. Where are we going? What are we going to do there? I wanted to ask, but I didn't. I took your money too, of course, each and every bill that you hid in the house, no, I withdrew it from our shared account. (Was there a shared account? Ha ha, of course there was.) But what would you do when you open your eyes in the morning and reach out your arm to hold me and I won't be there, I thought. Like all the mornings before that, of course: not hold me. Where will I be at that time? Where will I go? These were the kinds of questions I wanted to ask somebody for a long time now. I didn't ask them. Because this was a life that had suited me, and now I planned to unravel it.

The things I wanted to tell Assaf during that long drive and did not: I grew up in a wadi. They put the train car there because they wanted to live outside of society, though I didn't want that. In the nearby kibbutz they said I had lice and fleas. It's true, I had them. Once I reached behind my neck with my hand and found a small, unrecognizable lump. It was a tick, I realized. I took it off me. I brought it to my father, who squashed it with a stone. No, of course not, he crushed it between two fingers, and told me I was a little girl. The next tick I killed myself. Scorpions we smashed with stones. I grew up. I mean, how much did I grow? By this and that number of centimeters and this and that number of kilograms. It wasn't a pretty sight, but I got used to it. You get used to everything in the end, I wanted to say to Assaf, but he was quiet and so was I. What do you get used to? To precarious life, like that of the chicken that scampered on the balcony (What balcony? Was there a balcony?) until someone caught it by its neck and slaughtered it. It was served to the dinner table around which the family sat and ate, because had it not been for the table, the family would have been blown up. Assaf drove silently. Do you mind if I take off my nylons, I asked him. He didn't seem to mind it, so I removed them. I wanted him to look at my legs. They weren't a pretty sight, but when you love somebody you get used to everything. Surely you had. Then perhaps you get used to everything even when you don't love them. Because you didn't. My girl, my little girl, you told me. What girl? The one you didn't and wouldn't have with me. I cry sometimes when I wash the dishes, I wanted to tell Assaf. No, what I wanted to do was hit him. Aren't you ashamed!

he'll say, then hit me back. I'll drop to the floor. It'll hurt, no, it won't hurt me. Who decides it? Take a look at yourself, he'll say again, aren't you ashamed of yourself. I'll be ashamed. When I stand by the faucet my tears will mix with the soap water, and when I wipe them my eyes will burn. Someone will have to do something. I blinked. Assaf rolled his eyes. Isn't it dangerous to drive like this? For a moment I thought about the words you used to seduce me, who there was no need to seduce at all. They were black and hot and they incited me. In order to cool down I lay whole nights on the floor, and you stood above me and looked at me. No, it was someone else! But he still looked at my face for a while. Moved his eyes across my body. Held my palm with two fingers and said, Rise. What could I do? Nothing. I rose up.

Assaf drove confidently, and nothing, it seemed, made him tire. He did not look at me. I was very tired. I closed my eyes. Only when he left the car, to fill gas, buy more cigarettes, did I open them. Not wide open but two narrow slits, because now I didn't want to see more than his shadow. Was he a handsome man? In the news photos taken later he's seen hiding his face with his shirt, so until today I don't know. But I remember the heat from his body, and some kind of a strange vibration that he emanated. Without stopping. For long hours. Where did we go? Assaf, I thought, certainly has to pay someone. Or pick up something. We exchanged no words. This is what I wanted to say to him: if we go on driving we'll reach the end of the world, what's there? I might have mumbled something. Shhhh, said Assaf. Tonight's quiet. I shut up. I had more than enough time to think about what bothered me. What bothered me then? How even though I promised I wouldn't I left you alone in the world, each one of us and what they know best, and it wasn't very decent of me. What bothered you? Nothing. You left me to do whatever I felt like. And things that I didn't feel like. The sun shone. I got sick of sitting quietly. What is Karin's real name, Assaf, I asked. Karin, he told me. That's her name. What is your name? Justine, I answered. I didn't feel like anything. I left Assaf the bag with your money (mine, of course, I took with me). I put on my nylons again, buttoned my coat to the top, fasten my watch to my wrist. Assaf drove and drove and drove. I looked ahead, to the mountains, until I saw the familiar dusty road. Stop here, I told him. I'm getting out. He stopped. I turned back. I crossed the road. A car passed. The driver looked at me. What could I do? I didn't get in this time.

The dusty road appeared in my dreams. One right turn. Straight ahead. Another turn. What is waiting for me there? What's waiting is the horse I learned how to ride as a baby, the gun I shot, the lasso, the water under which I learned to dive deeper and deeper, let the flood waves wash over you. I let them. One could hope not to shatter. One night I spread the blanket on the floor in the middle of the living room (what living room, there was no living room), and all night long I dreamed and in the morning I woke up naked, even my underwear was gone. Growing up was a mistake, one that I cannot repent for. Though I tried. I searched for them everywhere, then I put on my pants without my underwear, and I ran out. They went searching for me. Who did? Everyone who had loved me: my mother, the kindergarten teacher, the pediatrician, the army people, the kibbutz members, the psychologists, the knife makers, the schoolteachers, the pedophile's son, the pretty girls, the first man who kissed me, those who wanted me to remember what they didn't want to remember themselves, my father. I remembered everything. Then I ran. Through the hills, to the crop fields, the pasture, to the mountains. I stopped for rest by the water trough, and there they besieged me. I held a stone and planned to hurl it with all my force at them, but in the end I smashed it on the side of my head. There was a lot of blood. When I woke up I discovered that I was spread naked on too soft a bed (there was no living room, but there were mirrors hung on the ceiling, and there was also a television that broadcasted—what was that?—pornography), and despite the man who lay on his belly by me I could notice that I was all alone (because remembering was a mistake and I was commanded to remember, so I did). I searched for the wound on my head and could not find it. Instead I found my underwear and put them on. I took out the small knife which I kept in my bag to be on the safe side and stabbed him in the thigh. In order to leave him something. Something to remind him of me. I left the money on the bedside dresser. Then I got out of there.

Someone

Someone wakes me up. Someone whispers in my ear, Shhhh, don't worry, everything's all right. Outside the moon shines, the wind blows. Someone hugs me, Shhhh, don't worry, everything's all right. Someone puts his hand inside my pants, don't worry, someone turns me on my belly. My eyelids are very heavy. Don't worry. Someone wakes me up. Someone removes my blanket and pushes his fingers in my mouth. Someone says, Shhhh, someone puts his hand inside my pants, under my pajama shirt. Someone grabs my flesh. No! Shhhh. Someone moans, Ahhhha, someone grabs my flesh. Everything's all right. Someone puts his head on my belly. Someone suckles me. Shhhh, shhhh, everything's all right. Someone takes off my clothes, someone calms me. My eyelids are very heavy. The moon shines. Someone puts his head on my shoulder, don't worry, someone strokes my hair, someone wraps his arms around me, holds me to his chest, someone says, everything's all right. Everything's all right. Someone looks in my eyes, then shuts them. Someone removes my underwear. Everything's all right. The curtains fly in the wind. I am not looking. Someone strokes me. Someone says, In the morning you'll forget everything. Someone strokes me. Someone says, Shhhh, my girl. My good girl. Someone calms me. Someone asks me to forgive him. I am not looking. I am not looking. Someone strokes my hair, moves my curls with his fingers. He's crying. He says: Everything will be all right. My eyelids are heavy, I am nodding. Someone puts on my clothes. The sun rises in the window, the curtains sway in the wind. Don't worry. So quiet here. Someone tells me, Shhhh, get back to sleep. Soon you'll forget everything. Someone fixes my blanket, kisses my forehead, says he loves me. Quiet here. Someone closes the door behind him. My eyelids are very heavy. I fall asleep.

Growing up was a mistake, one that I can no longer repent for. You could imagine, from up close, that these are real tears, on my two cheeks. But I don't cry. I don't cry, I told you, I never do. So you decided to make me cry. At first the pain surprised me. I made a fist and shoved it deep down my throat and screamed in silence to the empty space. Because this was exactly how I could scream as much as I wanted to. I gave up words, there was nothing left to say anyway. For a moment I might have imagined that something real would materialize from all the tears and the sorrow. A mistake. Truth was another commodity I had no interest in, like the books that were scattered between family and friends, the clothes that were taken out of the closet, the empty space that was left so there will be enough room for me and for you, but at the end left room only for come and for fury.

Flesh may or may not be touched, so I decided to touch it. At first only with the tips of my nails, then with my fingers, then the whole hand, and in the end I took a knife and I cut it. Who? My father, my best friend, the man I loved and who said he loved me. And then that he'd stopped loving me. Where did I go instead of lying next to you at night? To where one goes when the night falls. Or in winter when the clouds are heavy and tired and the sun sets, heavy too. For a moment I thought when I went to sleep that when I open the door the words will be there to climb them. Like the ladder on the roof of the house from my childhood. What house? There was no house. There was a family, or there once was and I forgot about it. Father and mother and a baby girl, so quiet one may think she's died already, on the bed in the morning light. A mistake. She was kept alive even after they'd killed them all, all of them. Who killed them? The one who cut the cattle fence with big metal scissors and let them escape. Where to? To the houses, beyond the fields. Where others could feed and water and raise them. In the meantime I peeked through the window curtains, what window? There was no window, I didn't peek, I wasn't there, but later I returned in Assaf's car and walked the dusty road, I walked the whole way back, and what I found were the foundations for the houses that had been abandoned before they were built, the old well, the water trough, a granary or a barn, and between the ruins, raising his hands, he stood.

I looked at him and got out of there.